Autistic Planet

Jennifer Elder

*Illustrated by Marc Thomas
and Jennifer Elder*

Jessica Kingsley Publishers
London and Philadelphia

First published in 2007
by Jessica Kingsley Publishers
116 Pentonville Road
London N1 9JB, UK
and
400 Market Street, Suite 400
Philadelphia, PA 19106, USA

www.jkp.com

Library of Congress Cataloging in Publication Data
Elder, Jennifer, 1968-
Autistic planet / Jennifer Elder ; illustrated by Marc Thomas and Jennifer Elder. — 1st American pbk. ed.
  p. cm.
ISBN-13: 978-1-84310-842-9 (hardback)
1. Autism—Juvenile literature. I. Thomas, Marc. II. Title.
RC553.A88E42 2007
616.85'882—dc22

                                                                              2006100073

British Library Cataloguing in Publication Data
A CIP catalogue record for this book is available from the British Library

ISBN 978 1 84310 842 9

Printed and bound in the People's Republic of China by
Nanjing Amity Printing Co., Ltd
APC-FT4954

For Paul

My autistic friend at school today

Made a perfect sphere of clay,

I asked, "Is that the moon?" but no,

She shook her head and answered, "Though

It may seem pretty strange to some,

This is the planet where I'm from…"

"In our world, all trains run on time

With kid conductors on the line,

People work in offices, where

Every seat's a rocking chair,

We don't do something one time, when…

…We can do it over and over again!

And each tot dreams of growing up

To make history at the chess World Cup.

Our love of music is so strong

That when we hear a great new song

We memorize each word we hear,

Go home, and play it back by ear.

There's nothing hot in 'aut' cuisine

Lumpy, gooey, brown or green,

The only foods to pass our lips

Are popcorn and potato chips.

We can't stand all that itchy stuff

Like clothes with collars, belts and cuffs

And if you'd let us have our way

We'd wear the same thing every day.

To our ears, talking sounds absurd

Unless we repeat every word,

When someone tells you, 'Tie your shoe,'

You answer back, 'Tie your shoe,' too!

If you'd like to be the mayor,

Our selection process is quite fair:

There are no votes to count, you see

You have to win the spelling bee.

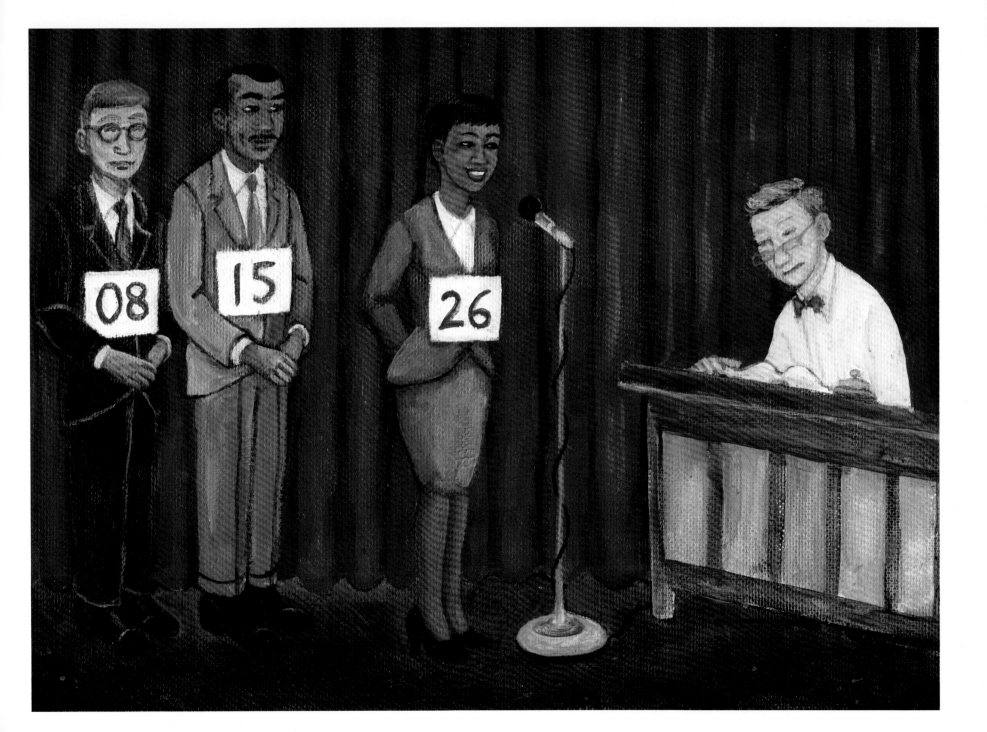

Of course, the TV news is short…

…We only watch the weather report.

And at the end of every day,

We flap our wings and fly away."

I asked her, "Is this planet real?"

And she said, "Well, it's how I feel,

And when your world spins out of line,

You're always welcome back to mine."

Further reading for children aged 5–9

Different Croaks for Different Folks
All About Children with Special Learning Needs
Midori Ochiai
With notes on developmental differences by Shinya Miyamoto
Illustrated by Hiroko Fujiwara
Translated by Esther Sanders
ISBN 978 1 84310 392 9

Can I tell you about Asperger Syndrome?
A Guide for Friends and Family
Jude Welton
Illustrated by Jane Telford
ISBN 978 1 84310 206 9

Further reading for children aged 7–11

Different Like Me
My Book of Autism Heroes
Jennifer Elder
Illustrations by Marc Thomas and Jennifer Elder
ISBN 978 1 84310 815 3

Praise for *Different Like Me*:

"This book will help inspire kids who are different and shows them that they too can succeed."

—*Temple Grandin, Associate Professor of Animal Science, Colorado State University, and author of* Animals in Translation

"…this is a great confidence booster for children with a 'high functioning' Autistic Spectrum Disorder, an opportunity for them to show off, and an enjoyable read for everyone, to boot!"

—*Education Otherwise*

Adam's Alternative Sports Day
An Asperger Story
Jude Welton
ISBN 978 1 84310 300 4

All Cats Have Asperger Syndrome
Kathy Hoopmann
ISBN 978 1 84310 481 0

Brotherly Feelings
Me, My Emotions, and My Brother with Asperger's Syndrome
Sam Frender and Robin Schiffmiller
Illustrations by Dennis Dittrich
ISBN 978 1 84310 850 4

Baj and the Word Launcher
Space Age Asperger Adventures in Communication
Pamela Victor
Cover illustration by Chris Shadoian
ISBN 978 1 84310 830 6